Ready for
adventure,
Kiddo?

Title:
The Adventures of AeroSquad Special Edition:
Vicky Viper and the Thunderchickens
Robbie Raptor and the Invisiloop

Author: Taylor Fox

Project Designer: Celina Milla

Publisher: Amazon KDP

ISBN: 979-8-9882483-4-7

Special Edition

Published: September 2023

For jet facts at the end of the book, data derived from:
U.S. Air Force. (2021, September). F-16 Fighting Falcon. Retrieved from https://www.af.mil/About-Us/Fact-Sheets/Display/Article/104505/f-16-fighting-falcon/.

U.S. Air Force. (2022, August). F-22 Raptor. Retrieved from https://www.af.mil/About-Us/Fact-Sheets/Display/Article/104506/f-22-raptor/.

For inquiries regarding permissions or to contact the author, please write to:

www.AeroSquadKids.com

This book is a work of fiction. Names, characters, places, and incidents are the product of the author's imagination or are used fictitiously.

For Pop,
the real Papa Jack.

The Adventures of AeroSquad

Vicky Viper
& the Thunderchickens
Begins on Page 4

Robbie Raptor
& the Invisiloop
Begins on Page 40

By Taylor Fox

The Adventures of
AeroSquad
Vicky Viper
& the Thunderchickens

Vicky Viper was the most energetic little jet in the world. She loved zooming and flying with her wing-buddies for hours on end.

But there was nothing Vicky loved more than watching the Thunderchickens as they practiced cool tricks through the clouds.

The Thunderchickens were the world's best formation team. Vicky would often catch herself daydreaming about flying with her sky heroes, creating stunning displays of aerobatics.

"Someday," she dreamt, "I'll fly with them!"

But, every time the Thunderchickens had tryouts, Vicky would always fall short. This year, young Vinny Viper was picked for the team, leaving Vicky feeling left out and disappointed. She was happy for Vinny but wondered what she was doing wrong.

Papa Jack was a wise old biplane that loved to nap in the hangar. Vicky knew that she could always count on Papa Jack for words of wisdom, so one day she taxied over to him for advice.

"Papa," she mumbled. "I need your help... I want to be a Thunderchicken with all my engine, but I never get picked to fly with them.
Is there something wrong with me?"

"There's nothing wrong with you, kiddo! Sometimes it's just not the right time. Let me ask, are you studying and practicing formations every day?"

Vicky gasped. The truth was, she always liked to do a little bit of everything - but playing with her friends took up most of her time.

She flew low through the mountains with Wiley Warthog,

played high in the sky with Robbie Raptor,

and breezed over the waves with Harry Hornet.

They would call her and ask,
"Hey Vicky! Want to go supersonic?!"
To which she would always reply,
"Let's zoom for glory!"

Papa Jack continued, "You see kiddo, if you've got a dream, then focus all of your engine's thrust on achieving that goal!"

Vicky nodded and thought to herself,
"Papa Jack is right! If I want to achieve my dream

I need to work hard, until the last drop of fuel!"

Over the next few months, Vicky focused on becoming the very best jet she could be. She woke up early in the morning and took off at sunrise, practicing formations every day, getting better and better.

She was even working on a new secret maneuver called the Swirling Falcon, where she would spin straight up into the sky near the puffy clouds and transform them into cute cloud animals for the airshows.

But, while she worked hard to form a cloud-*Dog*, she kept making cloud-hotdogs instead! Vicky looked at the sky and sighed, but she knew that giving up was not an option if she truly wanted to be a Thunderchicken someday.

Finally, the day came for the Thunderchicken tryouts and Vicky was very nervous. She rose high into the sky, her engine roaring with excitement. Vicky flew in perfect formation, creating the most beautiful displays of aerobatics with the team.

The crowds cheered from below. She had never felt so alive, but nearing the end of the tryout, Vicky knew she had to try the difficult Swirling Falcon. This was her chance to impress everyone with her hard work.

As she finished sculpting the cloud, she looked back down at it, beaming with pride. It was a perfect Thunderchicken!

The Thunderchickens were amazed–they had never seen anything like it. They immediately gave her a spot on the team!

As the jets landed, Vicky grinned from wing to wing. By focusing on her goals, she was able to achieve her dream.

In the distance, she saw Papa Jack taxiing to the hangar.

"Thank you, Papa Jack," she said.
"I couldn't have done it without you!"

"Look at you! You're a real Thunderchicken now!" Exclaimed Papa Jack, beaming with joy. "I knew you could do it, kiddo. The recipe for success is focus and hard work!"

The End.

F-16 Viper

Vicky Viper is based on the F-16 Fighting Falcon but F-16 pilots decided to give the jet a special nickname: The Viper. The Viper is an incredible fighter jet used by many countries around the world. It's like a speedy and agile superhero in the sky! The Viper is known for its versatility and ability to do many different types of missions. It can fly high in the sky and go zooming through the clouds, or it can fly low and fast through the mountains to surprise the bad guys.

Max Altitude:
50,000 feet +
More than 35 stacked Empire State buildings!

Wingspan:
32' 8" (9.8 mts)
About the width of a tennis court!

Max Weight:
37,500 lbs
Like 680 Labrador Retrievers!

Height:
16' (4.8 mts)
Same height as a double decker bus!

Thrust:
27,000 lbs
How many pounds can you push?

Fuel Tank:
7,000 lbs
1,044 gallons, like filling up a car 70 times.

Length:
49' 5" (14.8 mts)
same length as a Whale shark!

Top Speed:
1,500 mph
Mach 2, twice the speed of sound!

Cost:
$29 million
About the cost of 1,000 cars!

First Flight:
Jan 1974
Same year the Rubik's Cube was introduced.

Fun Fact!

When the F-16 turns, it can pull 9 G-Forces or 9 times the force of gravity to make really tight and quick turns in the sky. Imagine if you suddenly weighed 9 times what you weigh right now? That's what F-16 pilots experience all of the time! If you weigh 50 lbs, you would weigh 450 lbs! If your parents weigh 150 lbs, they would weigh 1,350 lbs!

How Good are your Pilot eyes?

1. Did you notice a cloud animal anywhere? What animal was it?

2. Pilots have to watch out for birds! How many birds did you see in the book?

3. Sammy Strike Eagle always wears his famous Starglasses, did you notice anyone else trying them on?

4. In every story, we include a real life fighter pilot callsign (nickname) of someone that flew with author Taylor. Can you figure out which word it is?

5. Vicky is an F-16 fighter jet, did you notice the number 16 in the book?

6. Did you spot the AeroSquad wing emblem anywhere?

Find answers at the bottom of this page!

Aviation Glossary

Aerobatics - Exciting sky acrobatics. Skilled pilots do loops, rolls, and twists with airplanes, performing exciting tricks and stunts.

Airshows - Fun events where people gather to watch airplanes performing exciting tricks in the sky.

Formation - A team of airplanes flying together in cool patterns. They work as a group, staying organized and performing amazing tricks, like birds flying in a flock.

How Good are your Pilot eyes? Answers:

1. Elephant, page 23. **2.** 21 birds. **3.** Robbie Raptor, page 18. **4.** Dog, page 25. **5.** Upside down, page 29. **6.** On tool box, page 14.

Ready for the next adventure?

The Adventures of AeroSquad

Robbie Raptor
& the InvisiLoop

Robbie Raptor was a daring little fighter jet. He spent most of his days flying with his squad, going on secret missions, and saving the world from danger.

The AeroSquad included Pedro Panther, Wiley Warthog, Vicky Viper and other amazing jets. They were all great wing-buddies and always had each other's backs.

Robbie was a very special fighter jet because he could fly at supersonic speeds AND become invisible to radar with his stealth mode. Whenever Robbie needed any of his special powers, he would simply yell,

"Afterburners Engage!"

This would activate his stealth mode, and his little engines would fire up, launching him into the stratosphere. Secret missions were his specialty.

But when it came to playing with his friends, they never appreciated his special powers. He could do amazing things, but nobody ever seemed to notice.

One morning, the squad decided to play one of his favorite games in the world – racing.

"Let's see who can really fly the fastest and highest!" yelled Vicky from afar.

Robbie was excited.

"Look what I can do, guys!" he whooped.
"Afterburners Engage!"

Like *Magic*, Robbie vanished into the clouds as he climbed at supersonic speeds. He was almost reaching the top of the stratosphere when he heard cheering in the distance.

"One more victory for Vicky Viper!"

The squad cheered because they had lost sight of Robbie.

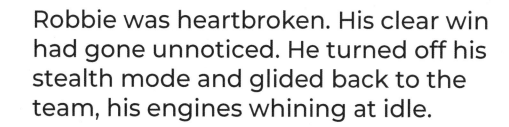

Robbie was heartbroken. His clear win had gone unnoticed. He turned off his stealth mode and glided back to the team, his engines whining at idle.

"Where were you, Robbie?" They asked.

A low-spirited Robbie replied, "I was just…
nevermind. Congratulations, Vicky."

Robbie sighed as he returned to home base, feeling alone. What is the point of being special if you can't show your friends?

Papa Jack, the old biplane, heard some sniffles coming from the hangar, so he taxied over to find the young Raptor tearing up.

"Aw, it's okay Robbie. What seems to be the problem, kiddo?"

"Why do I have this stealthy superpower if nobody can see me use it?
Sometimes I feel like I am invisible."

Papa Jack smiled lovingly. "I understand how you feel, Robbie. You want your friends to see your superpower, but it's still a superpower even when no one is watching.

You are amazing even if they don't see it.
Many heroes go unnoticed everyday."

Robbie's eyes widened. Papa Jack was right.

Just as the last sentence left Papa Jack's mouth, he and Robbie heard a scream.

"HelllPPP!" The AeroSquad was in trouble.

They were being chased by the evil Sky Bandits and struggling to get away!

Not on my radar! Afterburners Engage!
yelled Robbie as his engines roared to life
and he shot straight up into the sky.

Skoooooooouup!

Robbie's stealth mode allowed him to go unnoticed by the Sky Bandits. When he arrived at the scene, he took everyone by surprise.

"Stay away from my friends!" he yelled. He accelerated in front of them and created a huge sonic boom as he broke the sound barrier and performed his famous **INViSiLOOP** around the mean jets!

Shhhhhheewwww Kabooooom!

The shock wave from the sonic boom made the Sky Bandits spin out of control. Confused, they quickly bugged out once they could fly again.

"Oh, my stealth mode was on," Robbie winked.

The AeroSquad rejoined for their heroic flight
back home and everyone praised him, chanting,

"Robbie! Robbie! Robbie!"

That day, Robbie learned that real superheroes save the day, even when no one is watching. He had great friends who appreciated him, but their cheer wasn't the only fuel his little engine needed.

Being proud and loving himself was just as big of a superpower as being stealthy and invisible.

The End.

Photograph by: Bill Fauth

F-22 Raptor

Robbie Raptor is based on the F-22A Raptor. The Raptor is a super-fast and stealthy jet fighter plane. It has a sleek and futuristic design, capable of flying at incredible speeds and outmaneuvering other aircraft. The Raptor is equipped with advanced sensors and weapons, making it a fearsome air-to-air combatant. Its primary mission is to dominate the skies and provide air superiority.

Max Altitude:
50,000 feet +
Almost twice as high as a passenger jet can fly!

Wingspan:
44' 6" (13.6 mts)
The size of a humpback whale.

Max Weight:
83,500 lbs
Like 7 African elephants!

Height:
16'8" (5.1 mts)
Same height as a giraffe.

Thrust:
70,000 lbs
How many pounds can you push?

Fuel Tank:
18,000 lbs
2,686 gallons, like filling up a car 179 times.

Length:
62'1" (18.9 mts)
About the same length as a bowling lane.

Top Speed:
1,500 m/h
Mach 2, twice the speed of sound!

Cost:
$143 million
Like buying 715,000 bicycles!

First Flight:
Sept 1997
Same year Harry Potter was published.

Fun Fact!

Did you know that fighter jets are so fast they can fly faster than the speed of sound? When they break the sound barrier, they create a loud 'boom' called a sonic boom that can even break windows in a house! So, next time you hear your mom asking you to come to dinner, just remember, the sound of her voice is much slower than these incredible jets!

73

Was this on your radar?

1. Did you notice a cloud animal anywhere? What animal was it?
2. Pilots have to watch out for birds! How many birds did you see in the book?
3. Sammy Strike Eagle always wears his famous Starglasses, did you notice anyone else trying them on?
4. In every story, we include a real life fighter pilot callsign (nickname) of someone that flew with author Taylor. Can you figure out which word it is?
5. Robbie is an F-22 fighter jet, did you notice the number 22 in the book?
6. Did you spot the AeroSquad wing emblem anywhere?

Find answers on next page!

CHARACTER SKILL CHART

Robbie Raptor (F-22)

Speed ●●●●●	Air Support ●●●●●
Stealth ●●●●●	Ground Support ●●○○○
Maneuverability ●●●●●	Endurance ●●●○○
Versatility ●●●●○	Sensors ●●●●●

Wiley Warthog (A-10)

Speed ●○○○○	Air Support ●○○○○
Stealth ●○○○○	Ground Support ●●●●●
Maneuverability ●●○○○	Endurance ●●●●●
Versatility ●●○○○	Sensors ●●●○○

Vicky Viper (F-16)

Speed ●●●○○	Air Support ●●●●○
Stealth ●●○○○	Ground Support ●●●●○
Maneuverability ●●●●○	Endurance ●●●○○
Versatility ●●●●○	Sensors ●●●○○

Harry Hornet (F-18)

Speed ●●●●○	Air Support ●●●●○
Stealth ●●○○○	Ground Support ●●●●○
Maneuverability ●●●●○	Endurance ●●●○○
Versatility ●●●●○	Sensors ●●●●○

Pedro Panther (F-35)

Speed ●●●○○	Air Support ●●●●○
Stealth ●●●●●	Ground Support ●●●○○
Maneuverability ●●●○○	Endurance ●●●●○
Versatility ●●●●○	Sensors ●●●●●

Drogo Dragon (J-20)

Speed ●●●●○	Air Support ●●●●●
Stealth ●●●●○	Ground Support ●●○○○
Maneuverability ●●●●○	Endurance ●●●●○
Versatility ●●●●○	Sensors ●●●●○

Sammy & Sofia Strike Eagle (F-15E)

Speed ●●●●○	Air Support ●●●●○
Stealth ●○○○○	Ground Support ●●●●●
Maneuverability ●●●○○	Endurance ●●●●●
Versatility ●●●●●	Sensors ●●●●○

Melvin & Milton Migs (F-5)

Speed ●●●●○	Air Support ●●●○○
Stealth ●○○○○	Ground Support ●●○○○
Maneuverability ●●●○○	Endurance ●●○○○
Versatility ●●●○○	Sensors ●●○○○

About the Author  - Meet Taylor Fox

Taylor is a former fighter pilot with over a decade of experience in The U.S. Air Force flying the F-22 and F-16. Taylor's love for aviation started at a young age, as he looped through the skies with his former fighter-pilot grandfather, Papa Jack. When he's not writing books, Taylor can be found flying across the world as an airline pilot or hanging out with his nephews, convincing them to become pilots someday. So buckle up, put on your aviator goggles, and join Taylor, callsign Chop, on a high-flying adventure with the AeroSquad!

About the Illustrator - Meet Celina Milla

El Salvador native Celina Milla is the designer behind the beloved character designs in AeroSquad. Still a kid at heart, Celina has worked closely with children organizations throughout her life. Combining Taylor's keen eye for representing aircraft accurately, and her commitment to creating characters that all kids would enjoy, the AeroSquad cartoons were born.

Aviation Glossary

Afterburners - Turbo boosters for jet engines. Extra fuel is injected into the exhaust creating a burst of flames out of the back of the jet, giving them a powerful speed boost!

Bandit - A known bad guy or enemy.

Bugout (Bugged out) - The act of quickly and urgently leaving a dangerous or challenging situation while flying.

Radar - A gadget that works like magical eyes in the sky. Radars send out invisible radio waves that bounce back to find things far away, similar to the sonar bats use!

Sonic boom - A loud noise, like thunder, caused when airplanes fly faster than the speed of sound and break the sound barrier.

Stealth - A cool trick that helps special airplanes become invisible to radars and sneak around the sky without being easily detected.

Sound barrier - A special speed limit for airplanes that is the speed of sound. If a plane breaks this speed limit, it creates a loud 'sonic boom' noise!

Stratosphere - The high layer of sky above most clouds with the ozone layer that protects Earth. The air is thin and very cold.

How good are your Pilot eyes? Answers:

1. Cat, page 60. 2. 16 birds. 3. Pedro Panther, page 43. 4. Magic, page 51. 5. Top right, page 45. 6. Page 61, right side on the mountain.

75